BBC
DOCTOR WHO
TEAM *TARDIS* DIARIES

PAPER MOON
LOUIE STOWELL

PUFFIN

DIARY BOOTING UP . . .

WELCOME NEW USERS:

YASMIN KHAN

RYAN SINCLAIR

GRAHAM O'BRIEN.

PLEASE WAIT WHILE YOUR RECENT
MEMORIES ARE UPLOADED.

THIS MAY TAKE SEVERAL MOMENTS.

DOWNLOADING MEMORIES . . .

DATELINE:
WEDNESDAY 30 OCTOBER, 2019
EARTH

'Who got crumbs on the TARDIS console?' Graham brushed the offending crumbs away from the time machine's control panel.

The Doctor and her gang – Graham, Yaz and Ryan – were about to set off on a trip to the ocean planet Solarissa II, so that everyone could enjoy a nice rest on one of its many ocean-going pleasure cruisers. They'd raided the TARDIS wardrobe for swimming costumes, and they'd sourced packs of playing cards and books to read. The general mood on board was one of excitement.

Excitement, with a hint of annoyance.

'Honestly, can we try to keep things a bit

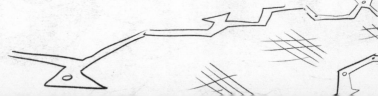

more shipshape around here?' complained Graham. 'I don't want anything jamming while we're midway between centuries.' He looked accusingly around at the others. 'Own up, who crumbed up the console?'

The Doctor looked up from her psychic paper and shrugged. She couldn't reply because her mouth was full of custard creams.

Psychic paper, in case anyone needs a reminder, is amazing stuff. It shows people what they expect to see, whether that's a Space Police ID card, a restaurant inspector certificate or an invitation to an exclusive party. In this case, it's being used to send a message by people who have a very special connection to psychic paper.

'I'm sure a few crumbs won't stop it working,' said Yaz. 'It's a time machine, not a laptop.'

The Doctor swallowed. 'Yes. No problem whatsoever. You're perfectly safe.'

'You always say that,' said Graham darkly. 'Even when we're being chased by giant robots.'

'Don't worry,' said the Doctor. 'This TARDIS has had a lot worse thrown at her than custard creams.'

Graham folded his arms and scowled. 'That's what I'm afraid of.'

The Doctor looked serious for a moment. 'I promise you, we'll get where we're going.' Then her face melted into a megawatt grin. 'Speaking of which, look what I just got.'

The Doctor lifted up her psychic paper, and showed it to the gang.

'Isn't this great?' she said, handing it to Graham, who passed it to Yaz, who gave it to Ryan. It read:

DEAR DOCTOR,

YOU ARE INVITED TO A FUNERAL.

THE ANCIENT HARDWOOD DAAL OF THE
DEEP ROOTS IS NEARING HER END.

PLEASE JOIN US TO CELEBRATE HER
PASSING, WHICH WILL OCCUR AT 08:00 BY
THE MOONCLOCK, DAY FORTY-EIGHT OF
THE NINTH CYCLE, IN THE FIFTY-FOURTH
CENTURY ON OUR MOON. MAY YOUR
JOURNEY BE EVER PEACEFUL.

YOURS IN GRACE,
THE PRODUCERS.

PS PLEASE WILL YOU RETURN MY COPY OF
THE WONDERFUL WIZARD OF OZ. YOU'VE
HAD IT FOR FOUR CENTURIES ACCORDING
TO MY LIVED TIMELINE.
IT'S A FIRST EDITION.

PPS THIS IS OLLA.

Ryan handed the psychic paper back to the Doctor after they'd all read the message. 'I don't get it,' he said. 'How come it's a funeral for someone who's not dead yet? And why are you looking so pleased about someone dying?'

The Doctor was indeed smiling a much-too-happy smile for someone who's just heard about a funeral.

'This isn't the kind of death you should be down about,' she said. 'Daal is one of the psychic trees of the forest moon of Boda, in the Plim Galaxy.

'I'm looking pleased because death isn't a sad thing for the trees of Boda,' the Doctor continued. 'They've always known the moment of their death, so they're at peace with it. This is a celebration of Daal's life, and it's a great honour to be invited.

'Plus,' she went on, 'the trees believe it's noble to die, because that way they can go on to help others, as *this*.' She waved the psychic paper at them. 'After death, the trees are turned *into* psychic paper.'

'WOW!' said Yaz, looking at the paper with new-found respect.

'Of course, it's not the tree any more,' said the Doctor in a thoughtful voice. 'The tree's essence passes on to wherever trees go when they die.'

'IKEA?' suggested Graham, which earned him a thump from Yaz.

'So, how does it work?' asked Ryan.

'The paper retains the tree's psychic properties,' the Doctor explained. 'And, I've got to tell you, this tree did *not* die in vain. It's got me out of more scrapes than you've had Yorkshire puddings.'

'Wow,' said Ryan, who'd had a *lot* of Yorkshire puddings over the years.

The Doctor pocketed the paper and went over to the console. She began pulling levers and jabbing at buttons, seemingly at random, but with the confidence of someone who trusted that the universe – and the TARDIS – would bend to her button-poking will. 'So, are you ready for a funeral, gang?'

They all nodded. Yaz looked excited. Ryan looked curious. Graham just looked a little sad.

'Yeah, go on,' he said. 'Let's go to a happy funeral.'

The Doctor gave a little nod and slammed a lever forward, kicking off the TARDIS.

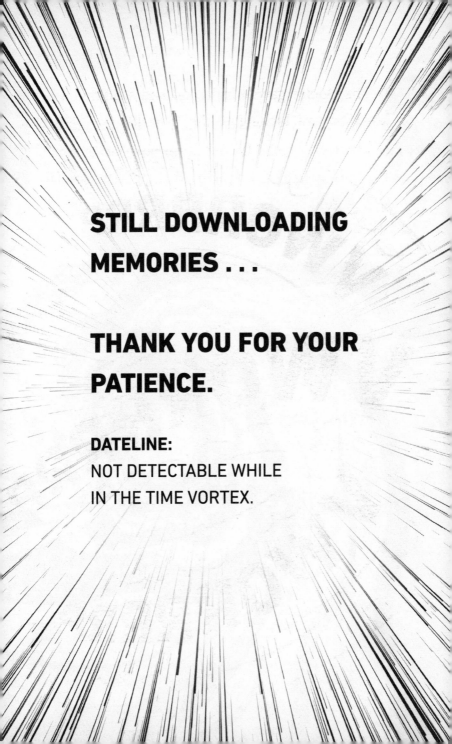

STILL DOWNLOADING
MEMORIES . . .

THANK YOU FOR YOUR
PATIENCE.

DATELINE:
NOT DETECTABLE WHILE
IN THE TIME VORTEX.

As they flew, the Doctor told them a little more about their destination. Boda was almost entirely covered in trees, except for a small clearing that was home to a factory. Not a smelly, polluting factory, but a quiet, clean place run on solar energy from the moon's three suns.

'Look.' The Doctor pointed to a map. 'Millions of trees, all breathing out oxygen. Prepare to feel extra-awake when we land. Even a bit giddy at times.'

The factory on Boda was run by a race of people called the Producers. 'You're going to love them,' said the Doctor. 'They're very chill. Except when you borrow their books for too long.'

'You didn't crack the spine, did you?' asked Yaz sternly.

The Doctor put her hand on her chest. 'Cross my hearts and hope to die. I may have made a few annotations . . .'

YAZ GAVE A
SHOCKED
GASP.

Look, I'm making one here, too, in this diary. Don't mind me. I'm adding notes from the future, when this story is over. No spoilers, though.

PROMISE.

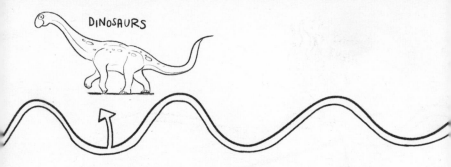

'Why are you invited to this funeral?' Ryan looked at the invite again. 'Are they friends of yours?'

'Great mates!' said the Doctor. 'Love the Producers. And their trees. We go way back.' She made a wibbly-wobbly gesture with her hand. 'And forward. I'm going to save them in the future, you see, from a particularly nasty species of bark-eating wasp. But, since the trees know what's to

WE MEET THE PRODUCERS

HUMANS INVENT FIRE

come, the Producers are already grateful. They gave me the psychic paper years ago as a thank-you for what I'm going to do for them.'

'This is doing my head in,' said Ryan. 'It's hard enough to remember what day it is when time only moves forward.'

AEROPLANES INVENTED

YOU ARE HERE

WASP ATTACK

'You'll get used to it,' said the Doctor. 'It can take a while to get out of the human habit of thinking about time like it's a straight line, and forward's the only way to go.'

'I just hope it doesn't break my brain first.' Ryan rubbed his temples. Yaz put a comforting hand on his shoulder.

'You always did find time hard,' said Yaz. 'Remember when we were in primary school and you used to sneak looks at your digital watch when we were supposed to be telling the time using the big hand and the little hand on the clock?'

'I didn't think anyone noticed,' said Ryan guiltily.

Yaz pointed to her eye. 'Keen observation skills. They don't let you into police school without them.'

JUST THEN, WITH A

THUMP,

THEY LANDED.

'Thousands of years old, and gravity always takes me by surprise,' muttered the Doctor. 'Never could get the hang of gravity. It's so bossy. *Up this, down that.*' She shook her head.

Gravity is the force, or pull, that keeps the universe together.

Don't worry, gravity, I love you really. I'd be a scattered mess of atoms without you!

'Now,' she said. 'Let's go and meet the Producers.'

'Who are they, apart from friends of yours?' asked Graham. 'They're not . . . film producers, are they?'

The Doctor laughed. 'No, not big fans of the movies either. They prefer books.' She pointed to the map with its spreading forests.

'The Producers are the guardians of the trees,' the Doctor explained. 'They're a bit like monks on Earth, only more fun, and with a few more arms. The Producers care for the trees while they live, and then create the psychic paper after the trees have passed on. Also, they make an exceedingly good afternoon tea. Come on! I'm starving!'

DOWNLOADING MEMORIES . . . THANK YOU FOR YOUR PATIENCE.

DATELINE:
DAY FORTY-EIGHT OF THE NINTH CYCLE, IN THE FIFTY-FOURTH CENTURY, FOREST MOON OF BODA.

Are you wondering what all this downloading of memories is about? You'll find out in a minute. Or, in the past, from my point of view.

Isn't time
BRILLIANT?

VWORRRRP

VWORRRRP

VWORRRRP

'AH, WE'RE HERE!' said the Doctor.

For once, the TARDIS was behaving itself. As they materialised on the moon of Boda, the Doctor gave the console an approving pat. 'That was smooth.'

The TARDIS made a last little **VWORRRRP** sound, perhaps in agreement.

'Why was it so smooth?' Ryan was always eager to find out what made the TARDIS tick.

'Let's just say, guiding a timeship with a mind of its own towards a moon full of psychic trees takes a lot less persuading than one that's just a ball of rock.' Not that there's anything bad about moons that are balls of rock. Some of my favourite moons are balls of rock. Including yours!' said the Doctor. 'Now, come on, we've got a funeral to attend!'

She strode to the exit and flung open both doors of the TARDIS.

The gang emerged on to the moon, where the air was full of the smell of leaves and earth. It filled them with energy as they breathed deeply.

'This smells so good,' said Yaz.

'I feel twenty-five again!' said Graham.

He saw Ryan's look. 'OK, thirty-five.'

Another look.

'Fine, forty-five! Anyway, I like the look of this moon!' Graham finished.

They'd landed at the edge of a clearing under a pinkish-blue sky.

To the left, trees spread out as far as the eye could see.

Some of the trees were familiar – ones that looked a little like pines, and others that looked like oaks. But some were completely unlike anything on Earth. One had spikes poking out along its trunk, like the neck-collar a punk would wear, which plumed up into pink leaves that looked almost like feathers.

'The psychic trees of the moon of Boda!' announced the Doctor. 'Hello, trees!' she added with a wave.

The trees rustled their branches, perhaps in greeting or perhaps in the wind.

'Come on, gang, let's head to the factory.' The Doctor pointed away from the trees to a beautiful curved building. It looked like a drop of golden syrup that had hardened after falling from the sky.

'What's it made of?' asked Yaz in wonder.

'Hardened tree sap,' said the Doctor. 'They don't waste anything here. The Producers are some of the cleverest builders in the multiverse. I once saw one of them make a battery out of some mud and a couple of sticks. Ah, here they come!'

The Producers were scampering forward to

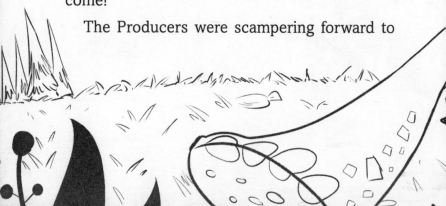

meet them across the clearing. Each was about the height of a ten-year-old child, and pale blue in colour. They had eight legs each and looked a lot like octopuses. But, as well as their eight legs, they had eight tentacle-like arms that ended in eight delicate fingers, all of which were waggling and waving in greeting. It was a bit like being welcomed by a bowl of blue spaghetti. Their faces had three eyes each, no nose, and a wide hole for a mouth.

'Many blessings!' said the closest Producer. The creature's face-hole rippled as it spoke. It bowed to the Doctor, then to each of the others.

'Many blessings,' said the Doctor. 'You look well, Olla. These are my friends, Yaz, Ryan and Graham. They're my plus one plus one plus one. Hope you don't mind.'

'It is a pleasure to welcome any friend of the Doctor's,' said Olla.

'Welcome to Departure Day,' said another Producer, who was a little shorter and rounder than Olla.

'Danar, how are you?' The Doctor bent to kiss the tip of one of the creature's tentacle fingers. 'How long has it been?'

'In lived time, far too long,' said Danar. 'Now, we have a moment before the Departure. Would you like some tea, and a tour of the factory?'

'Yes please!' said Ryan. 'I'd love to see how the paper's made.'

'And I could murder a cup of tea,' said Graham. 'If you have tea on this moon?'

'We have tea,' said Danar. 'Also, cakes.'

'Before we have tea . . . you're forgetting

something.' Olla tapped Danar on the shoulder with a tentacle digit.

'OH!' Danar slapped themself on the forehead. 'By the Nine Stars, I did. We have a gift for you, Doctor.'

'I didn't know Producers gave gifts at funerals,' said the Doctor. 'Is that new? I do like it when things change.'

It'd be weird if I didn't like change, wouldn't it? Considering that my whole face changes on a regular basis. And my body. Though, maybe one day, just my face will change, and I'll have the same body?

'This isn't a funeral tradition,' said Olla. 'This is a gift for you, from us, and from the trees. They told us that you might find it useful.'

Danar produced a book, partly wrapped in a protective cloth.

'It's a psychic diary.' Olla handed the book to the Doctor. 'It records your life as it happens, from your own point of view. It will take a while to download your recent memories before it starts working.'

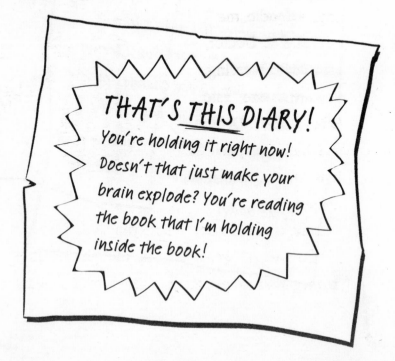

THAT'S THIS DIARY!
You're holding it right now!
Doesn't that just make your
brain explode? You're reading
the book that I'm holding
inside the book!

'Thank you!' said the Doctor. 'That sounds utterly brilliant. If you don't mind, I'll give it to my gang to share between themselves. I don't think the universe is ready for my diary. It might blow everybody's minds.' She stroked the book in its wrappings.

'Still, I won't promise not to doodle in the margins every now and then. Don't get enough time to doodle these days. Love a doodle, me.'

'Share it, Doctor, with our blessing. You are as one,' said Olla. 'The Doctor and their companions. It is known across the universe.'

'Hey, we're famous,' said Ryan.

'Are we . . . *good* famous, though?' A little frown gathered between Yaz's eyebrows. 'I mean, we're not on the universe's "Most Wanted" list or something, are we? I'd never live that down back at the station.'

Olla laughed. 'It is good. People tell tales of you, and the ones who went before. You should all touch the book in turn, so it can download your recent memories and get to know you all.'

Yaz, Graham and Ryan all touched the diary. It seemed to glow a little under their fingers.

LOOK!

It's downloading all their recent memories! The ones you've just been reading . . .

Yaz held out the diary to Ryan. 'Here. Let's see what the secret diary of Ryan Sinclair has to tell the world.'

'Er . . .' Ryan hesitated. He held it cautiously,

like it might explode or, at the very least, embarrass him more than a fart through a loudspeaker in a very public place.

'Unwrap it, and it will begin to tell your tale,' said Olla. 'Whoever holds it tells the story.'

'I'm not a good writer,' said Ryan doubtfully.

'This isn't that kind of diary,' said the Doctor. 'It locks on to you, and expresses your deepest thoughts.'

'It also has something of a personality of its own,' confessed Olla. 'So be gentle with it.'

Ryan gulped and nodded. He unwrapped it ever so carefully, taking the book into his palm and holding it like you'd hold a scared little mouse. The cover glowed red as he touched it. 'I think something's happening,' he murmured.

Oooh!
This is where it gets
REALLY good!

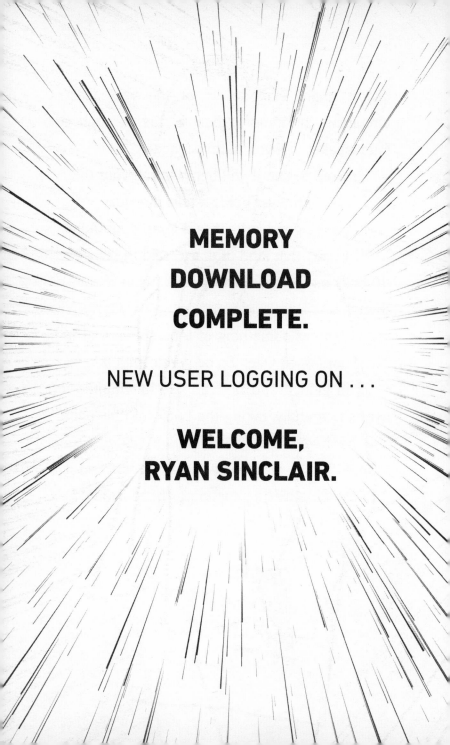

held the diary in my hands and it felt warm. 'I think something's happening,' I murmured . . .

Looking at the diary was freaking me out, so I shut it and put it in my back pocket. I really hoped I wasn't going to think about anything embarrassing while the book was writing down my thoughts. Like . . . that time I dropped a bacon roll on the floor and ate it anyway.

OH NO. Stop thinking, Ryan. Don't think about that time you turned up to school dressed as Spider-Man because you believed Keith in Year Six when he told you it was fancy-dress day, then everyone else was in their school uniform . . .

'Is there a way to erase stuff in this?' I asked, starting to sweat.

'No,' Olla said, in a muffled voice. I'm not sure, but I think maybe Olla and Danar were trying not to laugh behind their tentacles.

'Shall we begin our factory tour?' said Olla, gesturing towards the tree-sap building.

'I will leave you to prepare for the Departure.' Danar bowed their blue head.

We waved goodbye to Danar, and headed towards the factory.

Inside, the building was as beautiful as it was on the outside. The three suns were just visible through the tree-sap roof, making it glow.

We walked through a large reception area. It was like the ones you get in posh office buildings, with no furniture except a few plants growing up through the floor. And blue aliens, obviously.

'Are those plants psychic?' Yaz asked.

'Not unless they're keeping it secret.' The Doctor got out her sonic and waved it at the plants. 'Nope. But they are just about to flower. It's going to be stunning.'

I smiled. I can never get over how psyched the Doctor is about every little thing.

Nothing's little, Ryan!

Like, there was that time when I lost my wallet on a space station and someone handed it in and she acted like it was Christmas morning. I sometimes feel like a miserable old man next to her, even though she's, like, a thousand years older than me. Luckily, Graham's always there to remind me I'm not the grumpiest or the oldest man in this gang. No one grumps like Graham.

A new group of Producers scuttled up to us just then, holding bright yellow hard hats. 'Please wear these for your tour,' one of them said.

'Nice!' said the Doctor. 'I've been thinking it's time to get a new hat. Are hard hats cool now?'

'No,' said Yaz. 'Though you manage to look surprisingly good in that one, in spite of how uncool they are.'

'What are they for, though?' I asked Olla.

'They're to protect the raw psychic paper from your thoughts,' said Olla.

'What's wrong with our thoughts?' I was worried they were somehow tapping into the diary and seeing the bacon-roll thing.

'It's not personal,' said Olla. 'Just that the psychic paper isn't coated until later in the process. If you get too close to the raw version of it, you can permanently mark it, leaving it useless to anyone else. Look!' Olla pulled out a piece of crumpled paper.

What's for lunch?

I feel sad about the process of ageing.

Where did I leave my book?

'These helmets create a barrier between your thoughts and the paper when you're working with the raw stuff,' Olla explained.

'That's so cool. This place is so cool,' I said. 'Got any jobs going?'

'You should definitely hire our Ryan,' said the Doctor. 'Sharpest young engineer in the galaxy.'

'Trying to get rid of me, are you?' I asked, mostly joking.

'Never,' said the Doctor.

'Even if you wanted to leave the Doctor and join us, being a Producer isn't a job,' said Olla, in a very serious voice. 'It's a calling.'

'So . . . you don't get paid?' I asked.

Olla shook her head. I decided that, however cool the factory was, Nan would come back from heaven specially to tell me off if I worked for free.

The Doctor rapped on her hard hat. 'Everyone got their hats on? Very fetching, Graham, it suits you. And, Yaz, you look magnificent. Come on, Ryan, get it on you.'

I didn't fancy it much. Not a fan of wearing things someone else has been wearing. Like, what if they had head lice?

Gah, the thought made me itchy.

Still, I put it on.

'Excellent,' said the Doctor. 'Lead the way, Olla!'

The hard hats are specially designed so they *don't block signals* to fully processed psychic paper, only the raw stuff. So, this diary still works when someone's wearing the helmet, like Ryan is here. In case you were wondering why this page isn't suddenly blank.

If you were wondering that, *clever you!*

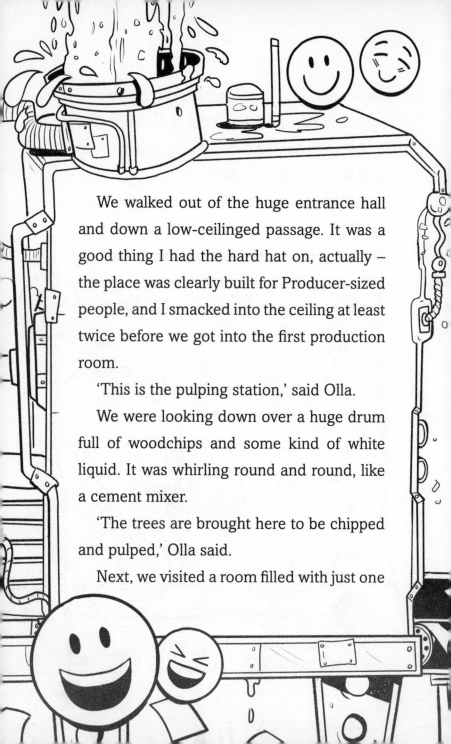

We walked out of the huge entrance hall and down a low-ceilinged passage. It was a good thing I had the hard hat on, actually – the place was clearly built for Producer-sized people, and I smacked into the ceiling at least twice before we got into the first production room.

'This is the pulping station,' said Olla.

We were looking down over a huge drum full of woodchips and some kind of white liquid. It was whirling round and round, like a cement mixer.

'The trees are brought here to be chipped and pulped,' Olla said.

Next, we visited a room filled with just one

giant machine. Wow – it was something else.
I got Olla to tell me all about it. I could tell Yaz
and Graham were getting a bit restless, but I
wanted to know the whole process.

SHORT VERSION: paste from the churned-
up trees gets poured in at one end and goes
through a pipe, and then out the other end
come sheets of flat, white paper,
trundling along a conveyor belt.

'After this, the sheets are coated by hand. Through here.' Olla pointed to a pair of sliding doors. We went through into a quiet room full of Producers. They were all sitting at little tables, with paintbrushes in hand. Danar saw us and waved a tentacle.

'What are they putting on the paper?' I asked.

'Anti-thought gel,' said Olla. 'It's the psychic equivalent of waterproofing. With the added advantage that it's also waterproof!'

'Brilliant!' I grinned. I couldn't believe I was walking around with this stuff in my back pocket. I couldn't resist getting it out and taking a sneak peek. The diagram it had drawn of the machine was incredible – totally accurate, but it also summed up what it felt like to look at it.

(I didn't know I mentally used that many emojis though? 😵)

'Do you make much money selling the paper?' I asked. 'I bet lots of companies are dying to get hold of it. You could make just about anything with it!'

Olla wiggled her tentacles at me, looking horrified. 'Oh no! It's not for sale. It's only ever freely given. We are protectors of the trees in both life and death, and you shouldn't sell what you protect.'

I felt ashamed, like I'd just been caught picking my nose in church.

But Olla smiled at me and I knew it was OK.

Good old Olla! The producers can be a LEETLE bit prim sometimes, but they're very kind. Always very kind.

'What kind of security do you have here?' asked Yaz. 'If your product isn't for sale, you can bet there are people who want to steal it.'

Olla sighed. 'Yes, that is the universe we live in. We do take precautions.'

She pointed to the corner of the room, where a number of figures were standing. I'd taken them for more Producers, but they weren't. They were Producer-shaped robots. Instead of a pale, soft blue, they were shiny, bright blue. Instead of soft tentacles, their arms were jointed like metallic blue caterpillars. They were, let's not lie, pretty **AWESOME**.

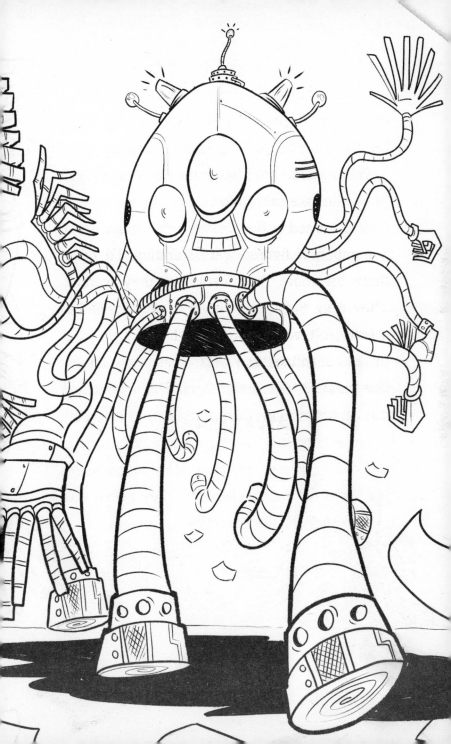

'We keep a few on guard in here,' said Olla. 'Then the rest patrol the edges of the forest. They're armed, but we've also taken the precaution of preventing weapons from arriving here.'

My eyes popped at the idea of that. 'What happens to the weapons?'

'They turn into harmless objects when they pass through our lunar forcefield. One team from the Kartomile Corporation tried to sneak in some guns but, by the time they'd landed, they were all just carrying Martian bananas. The looks on their faces when they pulled out their weapons!' Olla chuckled.

My favourite bananas grow on a planet called Villengard. There used to be weapons factories there, funnily enough. I didn't like them. Now there's banana trees instead.

WHOOOOP!
WHOOOOP!
WHOOOOP!
WHOOOOP!
WHOOOOP!
WHOOOOP!

An alarm sounded, and the Producers all slowly got up from their work, putting down their paintbrushes ever so gently, and bowing to the paper they'd been working on.

'What's happening?' asked Graham. 'Fire alarm?'

'I think it's time!' The Doctor was awestruck.

'It is,' said Olla. 'The Departure is upon us. Come. I'm afraid tea will have to wait. It is time to witness the death of a great tree.'

Outside, the Producers were gathered in a circle round a gigantic tree. All you could hear was their low chanting. Me and the others took off our hard hats and stood a bit away from the circle. The Doctor gave us a smile.

'The last sap is drying in the tree now. It's almost gone. **WOAH!**
LOOK!' The Doctor pointed to a butterfly that was flapping close to the tree. It just looked like a butterfly to me, but the Doctor seemed fascinated.

'A red admiral?' The Doctor exclaimed. 'That's not native to this moon. That's an Earth butterfly, that is!'

I half thought she was going to chase the butterfly into the woods – it wouldn't be the first time. But as the chanting of the Producers grew louder, I noticed a group of guard robots were forming an outer circle. They kept coming closer on their squirmy octopus-robot legs.

'Is that part of the ceremony?' Yaz asked the Doctor.

'Is what?' The Doctor's eyes were still glued to the butterfly.

'Er . . .' said Graham. 'That doesn't look very ceremonial to me.'

Now the Doctor was looking.

The robots had us surrounded, and their tentacles were pointed at us.

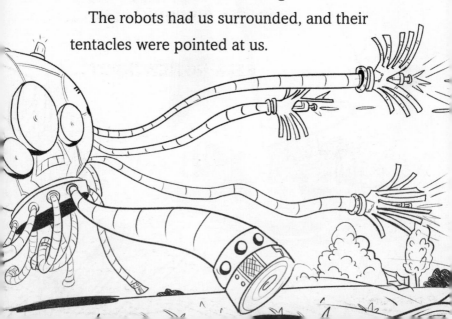

Tentacles which I could now see held blaster weapons.

'**RUN!**' yelled the Doctor, a moment before the shooting started.

I legged it. As I ran, I felt a shot whizz past me and I smelled burning close by. My legs pumped as fast as they could, and I kept pace with the others until my foot snagged a tree root. I stumbled, and could feel the diary slipping out of my pocket. I didn't care how precious it was, it wasn't worth getting shot in the back for, so I ran on.

DIARY DISCONNECTED . . .

SEEKING NEW INPUT . . .

I picked up the diary, almost without thinking, and ran. I tried to look for the others, but a blaster let off a shot so close by that I was blinded for a moment. I ran on, hoping I'd picked the right direction.

As my vision cleared, I realised I'd covered the distance from the edge of the clearing to the factory. The Doctor was beside me.

'YAZ – THIS WAY!'

She took my hand and pulled me through a door.

'Where are the others?' I gasped, looking back through the doorway.

The Doctor pointed. 'I saw Graham and Ryan scatter into the trees. Tried to go back for them, but the robots cut me off. They've got the Producers surrounded, over at the edge of the forest.'

Sure enough, the Producers were all huddled

together, surrounded by their formerly loyal robots. I felt a pang of guilt at leaving them behind. But at least Graham and Ryan had got away. I only hoped Ryan hadn't broken his leg on a tree root somewhere in the tangle of the forest.

'Someone reprogrammed those robots.' The Doctor was looking thoughtful. 'So, whoever's behind this is a bit of a whizz with technology. Can't wait to find out who they are! Come on!'

'Shouldn't we go and rescue them?' I nodded to the Producers.

The Doctor shook her head. 'Something tells me that they're not the target. I smell a diversion. Let's go this way . . .'

She started sprinting down the corridor. The Doctor loved nothing more than a good corridor sprint. I followed.

'What's the diversion from?' I asked as we ran along. I didn't know where we were going, but with the Doctor that was always half the fun.

'What's left unguarded with the Producers out of the way?'

The penny dropped. 'Only some of the most valuable paper in the galaxy!' I said.

'**BINGO!** Got it in one, you brilliant detective you!'

'You did give me a bit of a hint,' I pointed out.

'That's what I love about us. Back and forth. Give and take.'

The Doctor slowed to a fast walk as we came closer to the Producers' workshop, where they put the finishing touches to the psychic paper.

Outside the workshop, she put a finger to her lips, and I nodded. We both peered in through a window in the glowing-red sap walls. Inside

there were four people – human people – all
dressed in black.

'I'll give them this,' whispered the Doctor,
'at least they're wearing the right colour for a
funeral. Well, an Earth funeral. The Producers
don't wear clothes of any colour.'

'Who are they?' I whispered back as we
watched the thieves stuff paper into bags. I
thought about how Olla had told Ryan the paper
was only ever freely given. Well, now it was
being freely taken.

'No clue,' said the Doctor. 'Let's have a listen . . .' She aimed her sonic at the door, and suddenly I could hear everything that was being said inside.

> # I can't wait to spend the credits we get for *this* haul.

'Sonic extrapolator,' the Doctor explained. 'It magnifies the sound waves.'

Honestly, she could have said 'it's magic' and I would have believed her. Harry Potter's wand couldn't do half the stuff her sonic does.

I watched as the crew of thieves worked quickly and efficiently. They seemed to be having fun while they were doing it.

'Remember that time on Station Alpha K-70, when we ripped off that space cruiser?' said the dark-haired white woman.

'Good times, Zizi,' said the tall, skinny man. 'You bought that inflatable robot pool flamingo to celebrate!'

'Oh yeah, Ajay!' said Zizi. 'I loved that flamingo! You could float on it *and* it brought you drinks.'

'Did you guys hear something outside?' said the black woman, suddenly alert.

'I don't think so,' said the stocky white man with ginger hair and beard. 'Hey, pass me that pile, would you, Sue? My bag's got less than the others. Wouldn't want youse to hurt your backs.'

'Honour among thieves,' said Sue, breaking out into a broad smile and passing a stack of psychic paper. 'Or possibly you just want to impress the boss by bringing home more of the stash?'

The thieves were all wearing black hard hats, I realised. They'd definitely come prepared.

'Aww,' whispered the Doctor. 'I know what they're doing is wrong, but I do admire the team spirit. I like a good team!'

'Maybe we should stop the theft, instead of admiring it?' I suggested.

'Yeah, let's.' The Doctor fiddled with a cupboard in the wall, and brought out a couple of hard hats. 'Wear this. Don't want the paper alerting the thieves that we're coming.'

I nodded, putting my hat on. 'I saw a back door when we were in there. It was wedged open, so I think we can get in without them noticing.'

The Doctor turned her smile on me. Her eyes looked a little wild. It's easy to forget she's an alien sometimes, but when you see that look in her eyes, you know she's not from anywhere like home. And I don't just mean Sheffield.

If I was from Earth,
it would be an honour
to be from Sheffield.
Or Lagos. Always loved
Lagos. Don't go there
nearly enough.

'BRILLIANT!' she said.
'LET'S
GO!'

The door we'd passed earlier on our tour was still open, thankfully. I peered in. Just big enough for us both to squeeze through. We were shielded from view of the thieves by a large storage chest. I edged forward to look round it and saw the thieves were still at work. I realised they had a couple of robot guards with them, which were facing the other door. They were standing stock-still, perhaps awaiting orders.

'I guess since they couldn't bring weapons on to Boda, they wanted some firepower,' I whispered to the Doctor.

'Humans and guns.' She made a face. 'Worst love affair ever.'

I shrugged. She wasn't wrong. 'What's the plan?'

'Watch.' The Doctor strode out into the middle of the room, and I felt my heart leap up my throat and out of my mouth.

'What are you doing?' I hissed. 'They'll see you!'

Too late.

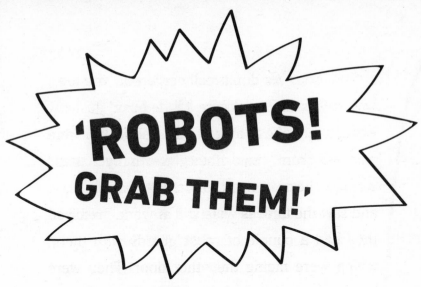

'ROBOTS! GRAB THEM!'

said the leader thief.

The robots scuttled forward on their many legs and grabbed us. I struggled, but the Doctor didn't. She just stood there and started talking.

'Sue, is it? You're in charge around here, right?'

Sue gave the Doctor a suspicious look. 'Who wants to know?'

'I'm the Doctor, and this is Yaz. Say hi, Yaz.'

'Hi,' I said, with a very pinched smile and a nod. The robot octopus had my hands behind my back so I couldn't wave. What was the Doctor playing at!?

'We don't really care who you are,' said Zizi. 'We're a little busy.'

'We should get the robots to shoot them,' said the ginger-haired thief. 'Then we can get on with the job.'

'Don't be hasty. I want to find out who sent them, first,' said Sue.

'No one sent us,' said the Doctor.

'Though we were invited. We're here for a funeral.'

Could I hear a faint noise? I could have sworn I heard something. A little buzz of something, very low, almost out of range of my hearing, like someone having a shave in the next room.

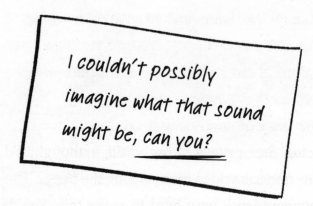

I couldn't possibly imagine what that sound might be, can you?

'Well, we're here to work,' said Zizi. 'And this paper won't steal itself.'

'Do you have to?' asked the Doctor. 'Couldn't you just . . . not? And say you did?'

'Or we could *not* not and say we did,' said Ajay. 'The boss is paying us big money for this job.'

'The boss? Is this like Beyoncé, where she only goes by one name because she's so brilliant?' asked the Doctor.

'Sounds familiar.' I couldn't help smiling even though we were in a messy situation.

'The boss is never-you-mind-who,' said Sue.

'I don't know what you think you're going to achieve by swanning in here.' She looked the Doctor up and down. 'How arrogant must you be, to think you can stop us?'

'Pretty arrogant, on a good day,' agreed the Doctor. She gave a shrug. 'Still, I thought I'd come and ask you to stop stealing the paper. The Producers work very hard to make this. You're taking something very precious from people who really care about their work.'

'We care about our work, too,' said Sue, with a quirk of a smile. 'We're professionals.'

If she hadn't been an intergalactic paper thief, I think I might have liked her.

'Come on, let's just zap them and get on with it,' said Zizi.

I did not like the sound of that. What was the Doctor up to?

'Was that the plan?' I hissed at her. 'Just . . . ask them to stop?'

'It's always worth a shot,' said the Doctor.

'Plus, keep people talking and sometimes, just sometimes, it gives you exactly long enough to reprogram their robots with your sonic screwdriver . . .'

'WHAT?' cried Sue.

The robots were loosening their tentacles. I could move my arms again.

Oh, you beautiful alien genius, I thought. She'd reprogrammed the robots!

We were free! I leaped back, and the Doctor waved her sonic in triumph. **THAT'S WHAT THE BUZZING I'D HEARD WAS!**

Yup, it was.

'I thought this moon didn't allow weapons?' Sue gestured to the sonic.

'Not a weapon,' said the Doctor. 'The only weapon I carry is this.' She tapped her head, meaning her great big giant brain.

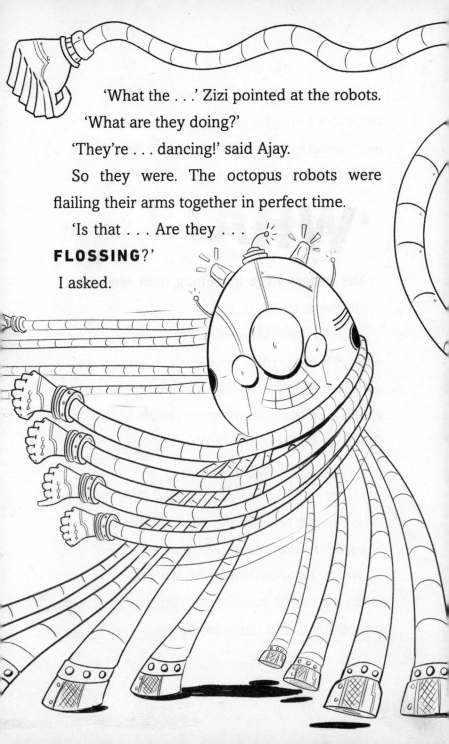

'What the . . .' Zizi pointed at the robots.

'What are they doing?'

'They're . . . dancing!' said Ajay.

So they were. The octopus robots were flailing their arms together in perfect time.

'Is that . . . Are they . . .

FLOSSING?'

I asked.

'Aw, you noticed!' grinned the Doctor. 'Did you know, in all the centuries and all the galaxies, that remains the *best*-known dance? Not always the best loved, but still. Can't have everything.'

The Doctor turned to the thieves. 'Now, if I were you, I'd drop the loot and get out of here! You don't know what else I've programmed those oh-so-funky bots to do.'

The thieves started to back away as the robots advanced. *I* knew the Doctor would never program those robots to hurt anyone, but the thieves didn't know that. They backed away, faster and faster, then they turned and ran, leaving most of the loot behind them.

'After them!' said the Doctor. 'We need to make sure they run all the way back to their spaceship – and then off Boda altogether!'

We raced after them. As we ran, I decided that, next time I'm home, I'm buying a big stash of energy bars to carry around with me. There's more sprinting with the Doctor than there is on the beat as a police officer. I was starting to get jelly legs.

The Doctor and I ran down a long, winding corridor. We ran down some stairs. We ran through a workshop full of strange machines that looked like a cross between arcade games and farm equipment. The thieves were just ahead of us at every turn, always slightly out of sight but not out of earshot. Their footsteps – and their angry voices – echoed down the corridors.

'Are we heading towards the exit?' I panted.

'Think so,' said the Doctor. 'It's just up that . . . oh.'

Ahead, the thieves had stopped. They yanked open a small hatch in the wall and climbed through. It clanged shut just as we got there. The panel read **RECYCLING CHUTE**.

I looked at the Doctor. She looked at me. It was decided without a word. We hurled ourselves down the chute behind them.

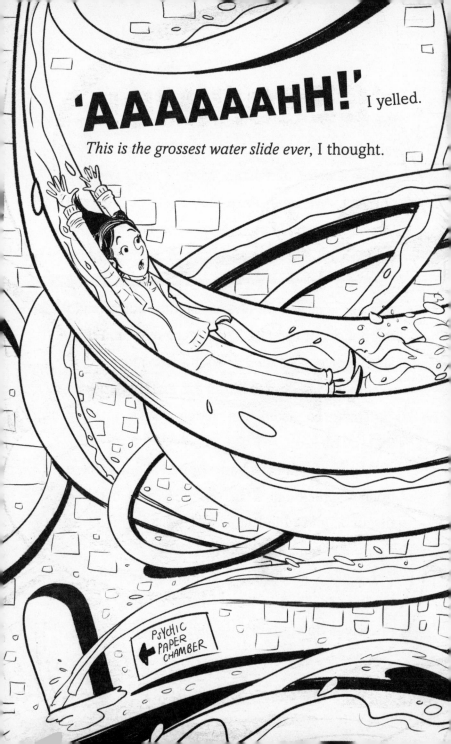

I could see Zizi ahead in the tunnels - at least I thought it was her from the trailing black hair. Just then, I saw that the tunnel forked. Zizi went down the left fork. I tried to angle my body to follow her, but a current of water rushed down the tube and nudged me off course.

We careered down the other fork, looping the loop. I could smell something ahead, like wood pulp, and I could hear a whirring sound.

'WE'RE HEADING FOR THE PSYCHIC-PAPER PROCESSING TANK!' the Doctor yelled.

'NO!' I yelled back.

'HOW DO WE TURN? WE'LL BE MUSHED!'

I glanced at the Doctor. We were slowing down as the tunnel flattened out, but I didn't think we could climb back up.

'Don't panic,' said the Doctor. 'We're going to be *fine*!' She suddenly looked very pleased.

In case you're not familiar with it, this is my I-HAVE-A-PLAN face.

My plans <u>never</u> go wrong.

<u>Rarely.</u>

<u>Sometimes.</u>

'Shouldn't we try to stop the blades?' I shouted, bracing myself against the edge of the tunnel. We were about to plunge into the pool of wood pulp, and the blades were turning faster and faster.

went the blades. They were close. And really fast. And really close.

I felt myself **SLIPPING**,

and then I was **FALLING**.

USER DISCONNECTED . . .

SEEKING NEW INPUT . . .

found the diary on the ground underneath a drainpipe, behind the factory. The fact it was there must mean one of the others dropped it . . . probably Yaz, given that Ryan lost it ages ago, and the Doctor didn't seem keen on carrying it.

That couldn't be good. Why did she drop it? Yaz was always very careful with her stuff. I was about to open the diary to read what she'd been doing when she lost it, when I noticed there were footprints going from the drainpipe across the clearing. Lots of them. Maybe three or four people?

'Here, Ryan, look at these.' I forgot the diary for a moment and absently tucked it into my jacket. 'Those aren't octopus footprints. Tentacleprints, I mean.'

'They look like human footprints to me,' said Ryan.

Ryan and I took off following the footprints, looking left and right. I had no idea where the Doc and Yaz were. Probably wherever the biggest trouble was. Maybe whoever made the footprints took Yaz and the Doc with them? Or maybe those footprints belonged to Yaz and the Doctor, and they'd made some new friends?

I doubted it though.

When the shooting had started earlier, Ryan and I had run off into the woods before we realised that Yaz and the Doctor weren't with us. By the time we realised, they were nowhere to be found. We sneaked back to check on the Producers, who had been surrounded by robot guards.

Ahhh, that's where Graham and Ryan got to!

They were trying to reason with the robots, but weren't getting very far. The robots just glared at them. I've met some nice robots in my time with the Doc, but those were not the cheery, fun type.

There we were, without a plan and no idea what was going on. Business as usual, then.

The footprints didn't lead to where the Producers were being held captive. Instead, they led through the forest – in a different direction to the one we'd taken before. We followed.

'Do you remember where we left the TARDIS?' I asked Ryan as we walked. 'I could've sworn it was parked in that bit of clearing we just passed.'

'Dunno.' Ryan shrugged. 'I usually just leave it to the Doctor to remember where we parked.'

'Well, hopefully we can find her, then.'

It was beautiful there under the trees. Shafts of light fell to the ground, casting strange shadows thanks to Boda's three suns. We saw some odd

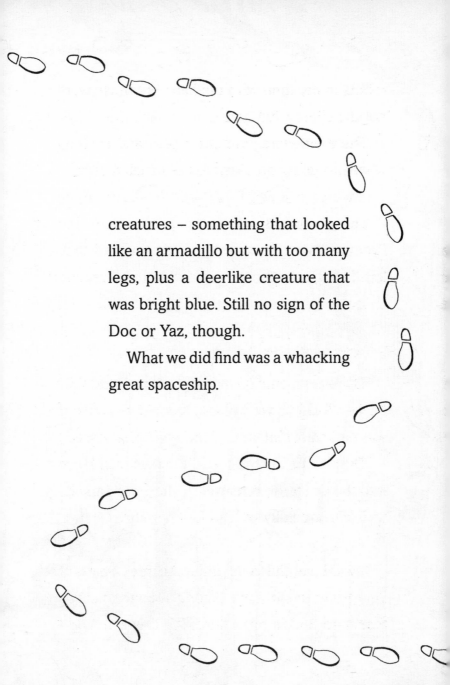

creatures – something that looked like an armadillo but with too many legs, plus a deerlike creature that was bright blue. Still no sign of the Doc or Yaz, though.

What we did find was a whacking great spaceship.

The spaceship was as big as a truck, made of rough, dirty metal, and shaped like an octagon. It was nestled among the trees in a clearing – well, a clearing that it had made for itself. I noticed a couple of damaged trees where the thing had come down.

'Vandals,' I hissed.

'Worse than vandals,' said Ryan. 'Those trees can think. Maybe they can feel pain, too.'

'What do you want to bet that the Doc's inside?' I pointed at the spaceship. 'She's always in the thick of things, after all.'

'Before we go and look, let me make sure it can't take off in a hurry.' Ryan inspected a panel in the side. 'I don't know much about spaceship engineering.' He paused. 'I don't know *anything* about spaceship engineering. But breaking a thing, that usually just takes common sense. And something to whack it with.'

He looked around and found a big rock. 'You keep watch.'

I nodded, and went round to the front of the ship. Which is when I bumped into four people in black. They were soggy and grumpy-looking. One of them had a piece of what looked like orange peel stuck in his hair. On the plus side, they weren't armed. On the minus side, that didn't matter much. I was outnumbered.

'GET HIM!' said one.

'I BET HE'S WORKING WITH HER!'

They got him. By which I mean, they got me.

They bundled me roughly up the gangplank. Well, I don't know if you call it a 'gangplank' on a spaceship. I'm going to have to get the Doc to teach me more about spaceships. If I live long enough to ask.

Depends on the spaceship. I think gangplank makes sense for this one, since this lot are basically space pirates.

Inside, the ship was greasy and messy – all wires and oily metal plates. Whoever built this thing didn't intend it as a luxury passenger ship, and whoever was maintaining it wasn't doing a very good job.

I hoped Ryan was succeeding at breaking it, because I for one did not fancy a trip through the freezing wastes of space inside that rust bucket.

'You like what you see, old man?' sneered a ginger-haired man.

'I've seen nicer ships,' I said. 'My friend the Doctor's got one that puts this heap to shame.' (Yeah, OK, on reflection I realise I could have been politer to the people holding me captive.)

'Sue, we've got a cheeky one here,' said the ginger-haired man.

The woman who must be Sue gave me a look. 'You insulting my ship?' She tutted. 'Fighting words.'

'Well, you have to admit, it's not exactly pretty, is it?' I pointed out.

'It gets the job done. Now, how about you

tell us more about this Doctor. I'm guessing she's the one who interrupted our little heist?'

'Sounds like her,' I admitted. 'She caught you red-handed trying to nick the paper, did she?'

It was a guess, but apparently I was correct.

'She could have lost us a lot of money,' said a miserable-looking woman with black hair.

'It's not your money to lose,' I said. 'You were nicking it.'

'A technicality,' said Sue. 'So, will the Doctor be following us, do you think?'

'She never gives up,' I said. 'She's relentless. If I know anything, I know that the Doctor never gives up on her friends.'

Aww, Graham, I just want to give you a hug through time.

Time-hug!

'Well, that's actually perfect,' said Sue. 'We'll just let her know that we have you, and she'll come to rescue you . . . and we'll make her hand over the rest of the paper in exchange for your life.'

'Too bad you won't be able to get away when you have the paper,' said a voice. Ryan had come up the gangplank and was standing in the doorway to the spaceship. 'You're grounded. I've made sure of that.'

'GRAB HIM!' ordered Sue.

The two men took Ryan and bundled him into the ship beside me.

'She has a ship, doesn't she?' pointed out Sue. 'The old man said so himself.'

'Less of the old!' I said. 'I'm in my prime!'

'Good luck with that! No one can take the Doctor's ship off her,' said Ryan.

'We do steal things for a living, you know.' Sue laughed. 'I think we'll manage.'

'Now that we have the two of them, what are

we going to do to get the Doctor here?' asked the miserable-looking woman.

'Hmm . . . Two of them . . .' said Sue. 'We only need one hostage to bargain. We can use the other one as a message – a dead message. Kill that one, and leave his body out in the clearing where she can find it easily.'

She was pointing at Ryan.

Yikes! I hope someone really good-looking and talented comes to rescue them very soon . . . this is getting tense!

'NO!' I cried.

'Robot, zap that one,' she said.

An octopus robot started skittering towards Ryan, raising one of its armed tentacles.

'Get away from him!' I shouted, feeling utterly helpless.

The robot's gun arm made a terrifying lock-and-load noise.

'DON'T!' I shouted.

But before the robot could shoot, a familiar sound started up. A beautiful, beautiful sound.

'**WHAT IS THAT?**' yelled one of the thieves. The TARDIS materialised, blocking the robot's shot. The blue police box's door opened and out came the Doctor, followed by Yaz. They were filthy, caked in white chalky stuff. But I could not have been more pleased to see them

if they were dressed in their finest party clothes and riding on white horses.

(I have seen them doing that, but that's another story.)

It's a really, really good story, actually.

They weren't alone in the TARDIS, though. A gang of octopus robots poured out, grabbing the criminals as they scattered out of the way of the TARDIS.

Was I going mad, or were the robots dancing as they grabbed the criminals?

When the thieves were all secure – tied up in a corner with some greasy ropes that the robots had managed to find in the spaceship – we had time to catch our breaths.

Yaz gave me and Ryan a hug.

'I'm glad we got here before anything bad happened to you,' she said.

'Depends how you define bad,' I said. 'I've been here ten minutes and no one's even offered me a cup of tea! I'm gasping.'

Yaz gave me a grin. 'Drama queen.'

I remembered the diary in my coat pocket. 'You dropped this.'

She smiled and reached out to take it. 'Thanks. We had a bit of a wild ride.'

USER DISCONNECTED . . .

SEEKING NEW INPUT . . .

slipped the diary in my pocket.

'What happened to you? You're all . . . sticky.' Ryan prodded my white-coated sleeve.

'We fell in a vat of tree pulp.' I brushed off a few damp wood shavings. It didn't help much. Man, I really needed a shower. But, on the upside, I was alive. So that was nice. 'I thought we were dead. When you get up close to those tree-pulping blades, they're *really* sharp and *really* big.'

'Glad you're both OK.' Graham had gone a bit pale.

'Wow. How did you escape?' asked Ryan. 'How did you get back to the TARDIS?'

'We didn't.' I smiled at the Doctor.

'We didn't get back to the TARDIS,' agreed the Doctor. 'The TARDIS came back to us.'

She always does, in the end.

'What, by remote control?' Ryan was forever trying to find out how the TARDIS worked, but the Doctor was always cagey about it.

I sometimes wondered if the TARDIS *changed* how it worked, almost like a person changes and grows. Maybe there was no TARDIS manual, because the TARDIS never worked the same way twice?

NO comment.
Well, except for this one, saying no comment.

'You remember how the TARDIS found it easy to fly here, because the psychic trees called out to her?' said the Doctor.

Ryan nodded.

'Well, it struck me – just as we were about to plunge to our very gungy deaths – that that might work for the pulp, too. So, a little boost with my sonic, and we were able to call for a lift.'

'The TARDIS appeared *just* as I was falling into the vat,' I said. 'It was a close call.'

'Aren't those the best calls?' The Doctor beamed.

'Wait,' said Graham. 'That's how *you* got to the TARDIS . . . how did you know to come *here*?'

'The diary,' said the Doctor. 'The TARDIS scanned for the current feed from it, and detected Graham's thoughts. Then it was just a matter of locking on to its location.'

'You read my diary?' Graham looked faintly offended.

'What, and you didn't flip back and read my pages?' I said.

'No, I'm a gentleman. By which I mean, I didn't have time.' Graham gave me a grin.

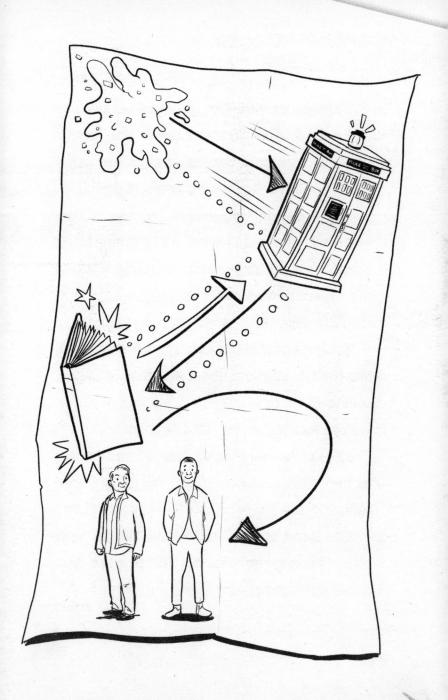

'Anyway,' said the Doctor. 'Here we are, safe and sound. And slightly mucky.' She looked down at her pulp-soaked clothes. 'Is wood pulp cool now? Can we make it a thing?'

'Let's decide the trends of the future when we've decided what we're going to do about *them*,' I suggested, nodding towards the thieves, who were glaring at us from their corner.

'I don't know about you, but I'd very much like to find out more about this boss of theirs,' said the Doctor.

'You said it, Doctor,' said Graham.

The Doctor didn't react; she just strode over to the thieves, coat swirling. We all gathered round.

'So, come on. Spill the beans. Who *is* your boss?' asked the Doctor. 'Who were you stealing the paper for?'

'Honestly?' said Sue. She looked very tired, and gave a big sigh. I saw this on the job a lot. There comes a time when a criminal knows there's no point fighting back, and they just sort of sag. 'Doesn't matter now. We're not getting our score, are we? But, as to who the boss really is . . . We don't know.'

'We've only ever communicated with them in code,' said Zizi.

'Really complicated code,' grumbled the ginger one. I still didn't know his name.

'We got the tip-off about the job at Andy's Bar, in the Delta quadrant of the Narkon Galaxy,' said Sue.

'Ah, love that bar,' said the Doctor. 'Go on . . .'

'A star pirate from the area told us about this boss, the Red Admiral, who was putting together a job, and she gave us the codes. She couldn't do the job herself as her ship was out of order, and she owed us a favour so . . .' Sue shrugged. 'Here we are.'

'The Red Admiral?' The Doctor's ears pricked up at that. 'Well, isn't that interesting?'

'Naming yourself after a butterfly? That's not so tough,' said Graham.

'Depends on the butterfly,' said the Doctor. 'The poison-winged butterflies of the planet Kadarantian are not to be sniffed at. Still . . . the Red Admiral.' She shook her head.

'Wasn't that the butterfly we saw earlier? The one that doesn't belong on this planet?' I asked.

'Yes.' The Doctor's face grew unusually still and thoughtful. 'What are the chances of that? Unless we brought it with us on the TARDIS. But she would have told me if we had a hitch-hiker. Hmm . . .'

I must check in the TARDIS's records if we had a flappy little guest on our trip from Earth. Because otherwise . . . what was it doing there? And it can't be a coincidence that the boss is called that, can it?

'Why's she so obsessed with some butterfly?' asked Ajay.

'She gets like that a lot,' said Graham. 'But maybe you shouldn't criticise someone's flights of fancy when they've got you bang to rights for grand larceny?'

'Grand what?' asked Ryan.

'Nicking stuff,' said Graham. 'A lot of stuff.'

The thieves scowled, but they didn't ask any more questions. I kept an eye on them, just in case their bonds weren't tight enough. An octopus robot was standing guard, too, boogeying a little.

It reminded me of something. Something we'd forgotten.

'Er, Doctor,' I said. 'The Producers! They're still penned in by the other octopus robots!'

'**YIKES!** Good thinking, Yaz. Unless you two had time to rescue them?' the Doctor asked Graham and Ryan.

'Been a bit busy being kidnapped,' admitted Graham.

'LET'S GO AND FREE THEM!

We can come back for this lot later.' She turned to the robots. 'Keep them safe and don't let them escape. And, if you get bored, dance at them. Maybe a bit of ballet next time?' She looked at me, then. 'One of these days I have to take you to see the robot ballet company of seventy-ninth-century Moscow. Beautiful!'

Leaving the thieves in the hands – or tentacles – of the robots, we trooped off through the forest to the clearing. It didn't take the Doctor long to reprogram the other robots to stop pointing their weapons at the Producers.

'Thank you, Doctor!' said Olla, when the Producers were all freed.

'We owe you our lives,' said Danar.

'That's OK ,' said the Doctor. 'I owe my life to a lot of people. So, let's just say, we all pay it forward.'

'That we do. But blessings be upon you, Doctor, and on your friends,' said Olla. 'But, might I ask, what happened? Who did this?'

'How about we tell you over tea?' suggested the Doctor. 'First . . . shall we complete the funeral?'

After the funeral was over (it was beautiful, by the way) we went inside the factory and had something to eat and drink. There were cups of tea like you get on Earth – in fact, exactly like you get in Yorkshire, which I did think was odd until the Doctor explained that, being psychic, the trees were able to tell the Producers the tastes of visitors in advance. They even had chai, and the sweets my grandma makes, too. Plus sandwiches and cakes and pretty much everything you could want to eat after a hard day's nearly-getting-pulped.

I chatted to Danar while the Doctor entertained the other Producers with a very long and complicated joke involving space–time and gravity that was way over all our heads.

I'm reading a great book about anti-gravity at the moment. I literally can't put it down.

'One thing I don't get,' I said to Danar, 'is why the trees didn't know the thieves were coming? If they're psychic?'

Danar waved a tentacle. 'They don't actually read the future, generally. Just their own destinies. Most of their psychic energy is focused on the present – where all our minds should be.'

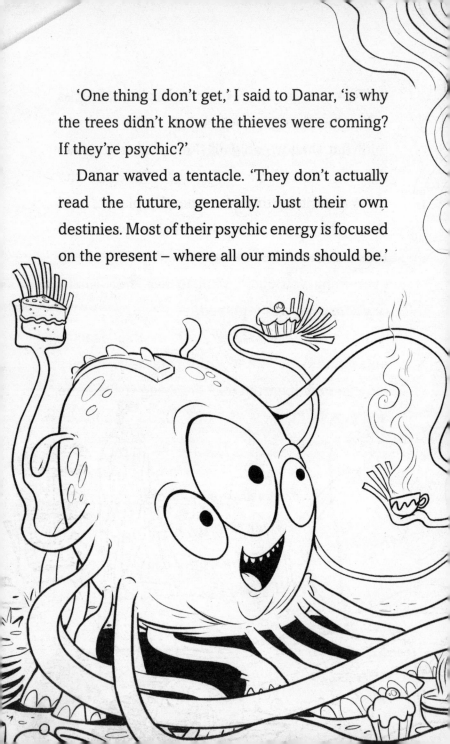

That was deep, and I chewed on my sweet as I thought about it.

'What shall we do with the prisoners?' asked Ryan.

'We will take them to a nearby planet,' said Olla. 'They have a very fair justice system and the thieves will be treated well.'

'One of those places with cushy prisons?' asked Graham disapprovingly.

Olla looked shocked. 'Prisons? Oh no. That's not justice. That's revenge. No, on the planet Tula VII, justice means doing something good as penance for something harmful.'

Graham frowned. 'How do you make bad people do good things without forcing them, though?'

'There's no such thing as bad people,' said Olla. 'Just people who have lost their way.'

Have I mentioned that I love Olla?

I thought that was beautiful, even though I wasn't sure I believed it was true.

The Doctor was nodding approvingly. She'd finished her joke and was leaning in to our little huddle. 'Never too late to change. I had a . . . friend once.

'He . . . she,' the Doctor went on, 'she made out like she was rotten to the core. But I know, deep down, she was magnificent. Her name was Missy. You'd like her. Well, you might. She was an acquired taste.'

The Doctor looked sad for a moment. It didn't feel right, seeing her like that. I just wanted to give her a hug, but I wasn't sure she wanted one in that moment, so we all just ate cake and talked about other stuff.

Isn't Yaz so nice?

'Olla, thank you so much for this diary,' I said. I had it in my hands, open at an earlier page, from the moment before the TARDIS rescued us. I still couldn't handle reading the 'live' page. It made me feel dizzy. But it was amazing being able to see into your own mind – in the past and in the present – and seeing your fears spread out in words – and pictures, too.

'I feel guilty keeping it as it's worth so much. Are you sure you don't need it back?' I asked.

I started passing it over to Olla, who pushed my hand gently away with a warm tentacle.

'Shh, no, you must keep it. The trees don't give these things idly. There will be a reason. After all, hasn't it saved your life already?'

I nodded.

'I hope it will tell you more about yourself, too,' Olla went on. 'Some truth your soul needs. Or some truth that will even save the world, perhaps?'

'I hope so,' I said. 'The world does need a lot of saving.'

'I can't wait to read the diary,' said the Doctor. 'If you all don't mind? I'll keep my hard hat on so I don't make it fritz out . . .'

'Depends,' said Graham. 'I'd need to read

back over it first, make sure there's nothing private.'

The Doctor nodded. 'Course. So, gang, hasn't this been a day? Haven't had a day like this in . . . **OOH** . . . **DAYS**!'

'True story, Doctor,' I said. 'And, there's something I need – when we've finished tea.'

'NAME IT!' said the Doctor.

'A shower,' I said. 'I'm so sticky, it's disgusting.'

Everyone laughed at that.

'And, after that, I want to go home and water my plants and have a good rest.'

'I think that can be arranged,' said the Doctor. 'Everyone finished their tea?'

Ryan shoved a couple of extra cakes in his pocket. The boy has hollow legs.

'Right, let's get going then,' said Graham. 'Yaz, can I take the diary to read over and check I'm OK with the Doc reading it? You two can do the same, obviously.'

'I'm good,' I said. 'I always speak my mind anyway.'

'Er, same,' said Ryan, though he looked a little more worried. 'Well, maybe I'll take a quick look . . . hard hat on, so it's in read-only mode . . .'

That's how I've been adding notes without taking over the diary. Plus, it's a very fetching hat, don't you think?

'Thanks for the tea, Olla,' I said.

'Thanks for everything,' said Olla.

We all hugged Olla, Danar and a few other Producers I'd never met before. They're friendly, those Producers. I was going to miss them.

'Can I borrow the diary for the trip home?' Ryan asked me. 'I'll give it to you next, Graham.'

'Sure!' I held out the diary to him.

USER DISCONNECTED . . .

SEEKING NEW INPUT . . .

We said goodbye to the Producers after tea and headed back to the TARDIS. I breathed in that fresh moon air one last time. Too fresh for me, really. I need a bit of city stink.

As we pushed into the blue box, I sidled up to the Doctor, who was at the console, preparing to leave.

'Doctor, will you just hold it for a minute and think about how the TARDIS works?' I pleaded. I waved the diary at her. 'Or hold it while you're piloting? I want to see if it can explain it to me?'

The Doctor didn't turn from her tappings, but she did frown a little. 'I can't promise I won't break it. And like Yaz said, it's a very precious object.'

'If it looks like it's going wrong, I'll snatch it away quick – I promise,' I said.

'Go on, then. Never say never.' She held out a hand. 'But keep touching it. Hopefully your consciousness will help tone down my effect on the thing.'

She flipped a switch on the TARDIS controls

with her other hand, and we lurched into motion. I carefully placed the book in her outstretched hand.

As the Doctor piloted the ship, the diary started to change.

I am in the **UNIVERSE**.
I am in the **NOW**.
I am in the **PAST**.

ALL MY SELVES are within me.
My hand on the controls. **HIS HAND.**
And his hand. And his, back to the beginning.

I STOLE HER, AND SHE IS MINE.

THE BUTTERFLY.
Where does the butterfly fit into this?

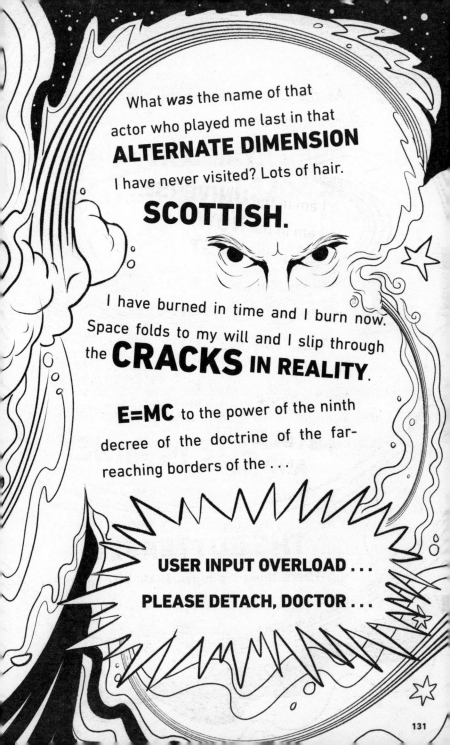

What *was* the name of that actor who played me last in that **ALTERNATE DIMENSION** I have never visited? Lots of hair.

SCOTTISH.

I have burned in time and I burn now. Space folds to my will and I slip through the **CRACKS IN REALITY**.

E=MC to the power of the ninth decree of the doctrine of the far-reaching borders of the . . .

USER INPUT OVERLOAD . . .

PLEASE DETACH, DOCTOR . . .

USER RYAN SINCLAIR IN SOLE CONTROL . . .

I grabbed the diary back, as the thing started to vibrate and curl at the edges, as though it was burning.

'Told you,' said the Doctor. 'But, I do like an experiment.' She pointed her sonic at the diary and scanned. 'No permanent damage, phew. But, from now on, I only touch it with my hat on, in read-only mode, right?'

We all nodded.

We flew the rest of the way back to Earth in relative calm. We'd decided to take a few days on Earth to see people, then head off to the cruise we'd been planning before the whole funeral–heist thing happened.

I was really ready for some relaxation. I could tell Graham was, too. The man looked grey with exhaustion. As we materialised on Earth, I held out the diary to him.

'See you all in a few days,' he said.

USER DISCONNECTED . . .

SEEKING NEW INPUT . . .

DATELINE:
THURSDAY 31 OCTOBER, 2019
EARTH

Home at last! Spent the day catching up on chores. Watered the plants. Cooked. Met a mate to play darts. Checked in on Yaz and Ryan. Felt glad to be home. I love travelling the galaxy and that, but there's no place like home.

I don't have a lot of thoughts, do I? Flipping back over the others' entries, those kids do a lot of thinking. Is it because I'm old? Or because I'm sad?

I'm still sad, a little bit every day. I miss her, you know?

It's still good to be home though.

DATELINE:
THURSDAY 31 OCTOBER, 2019
EARTH

Got up and pottered around. Made coffee. Had breakfast. Then I decided to spend some time reading over my parts of the diary, to check there wasn't anything I didn't want the Doctor reading. I didn't read Ryan or Yaz's entries. It felt wrong, somehow, prying like that. Though I did read the Doc's and, wow, being in that head of hers must be something else!

After coffee and reading, I glanced at yesterday again. Then I looked at today.

Then I realised something funny was going on, and called the Doctor right away.

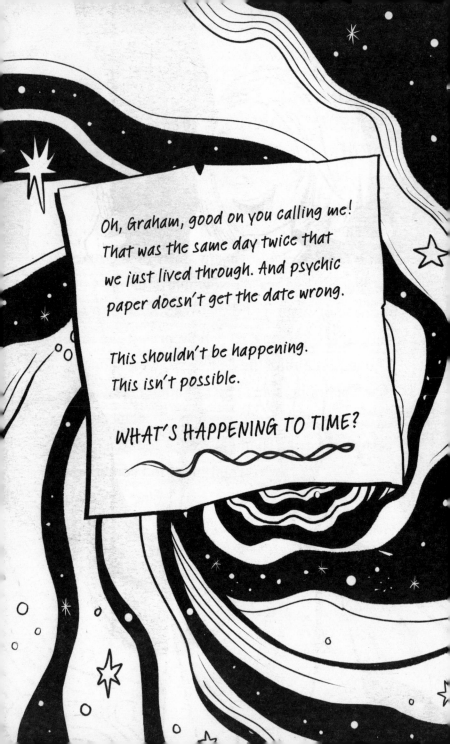